13887

DANVERS TOWNSHIP LIBRARY

P9-CRZ-431

A31300 047264

DATE DUE

JUL 1 1 1990	DEC. 0 2 1994	MAR 0 3 1999
JUL 1 6 1990	MAY 20 1995	JUL 0 8 1999
JUL 2 6 1990	SEP 3 0 1995	JUL 2 7 1999
AUG 0 3 1990	MAR. 2 2 1996	JUL 0 6 2001
OCT. 3 0 1991	JUN 2 5 1996	
NOV. 2 8 1991	JUL 1 9 1996	SEP 2 3 2004
AUG 0 7 1992	AUG 2 0 1996	SEP 1 6 2005
AUG 2 2 1992	DEC. 2 0 1996	APR 0 8 2011
AUG 2 5 1992	MAR 0 7 1997	
FEB. 1 0 1994	AUG 0 1 1997	
FEB. 2 1994	NOV 2 5 1997	
AUG 0 6 1994	JUL 0 3 1998	

DISCARD

E
Gay   Gay, Michel
          Take me for a ride

DANVERS TWP. LIBRARY
105 South West Street
Danvers, Illinois 61732
Phone: 963-4269

For Biboundé

Copyright © 1983 by L'ecole des Loisirs.
Published in France under the title *Pousse-Poussette*. All rights reserved. No part of this book may be reproduced or utilized in any form or by any means, electronic or mechanical, including photocopying, recording or by any information storage and retrieval system, without permission in writing from the Publisher. Inquiries should be addressed to William Morrow and Company, Inc., 105 Madison Avenue, New York, N.Y. 10016. Printed in the United States of America.   1 2 3 4 5 6 7 8 9 10

Library of Congress Cataloging in Publication Data
Gay, Michel. Take me for a ride.   Translation of: Pousse-poussette.   Summary: A little boy finds it hard to push his stroller as more and more animals get in for a ride. 1. Children's stories, French. I. Title. PZ7.G238Tak 1985   [E]   84-19088
ISBN 0-688-04135-3
ISBN 0-688-04136-1 (lib. bdg.)

MICHEL GAY

Take Me for a Ride

DANVERS TWP. LIBRARY
105 South West Street
Danvers, Illinois 61732
Phone: 963-4269

WILLIAM MORROW & COMPANY
NEW YORK

A butterfly sat down
on Teddy's stroller.

"How about a ride?" said Teddy. "Hold on, Butterfly."

Hop. Hop.

"How about me?"

"Hop in, Frog," said Teddy.

DANVERS TWP. LIBRARY
105 South West Street
Danvers, Illinois 61732
Phone: 963-4269

Quack. Quack. "What about me?
I want a ride, too."

"All aboard, Duck," said Teddy.

Meow. Meow. "It's my turn now."

"Cut it out, Pussycat," said Teddy.

DANVERS TWP. LIBRARY
105 South West Street
Danvers, Illinois 61732
Phone: 963-4269

"Hey, I didn't know you were there."

"I'm too tired to push you, too, Fox," said Teddy.

O-o-o-o-o-o. "Look out below!"

"Poor Bear. You hurt your tail," said Teddy.

"Faster, faster," said the bear.

But Teddy was going slower.

DANVERS TWP. LIBRARY
105 South West Street
Danvers, Illinois 61732
Phone: 963-4269

"Bear, Fox, Pussycat,
Duck, Frog, Butterfly . . .
where are you?"

"Here we are. . ."

". . .and away we go."

"Hey, not so fast!" said Teddy.

Wheeee!!!!

DANVERS TWP. LIBRARY
105 South West Street
Danvers, Illinois 61732
Phone: 963-4269

"Bye-bye, everybody.
Thanks for the ride."

"Who needs a big hug?" said Mommy.

"Come on, let's go for a ride."